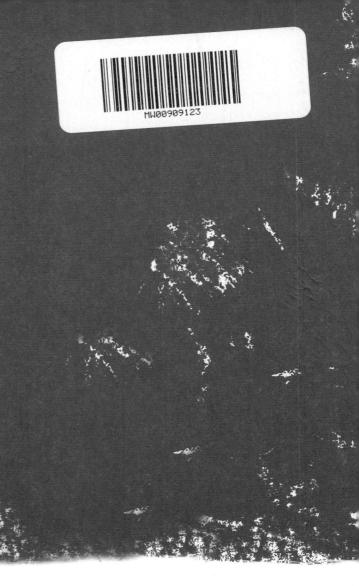

The Little Book of
DAD

Introduction

He is a playmate, an accomplice in the silly pranks that children play to put a big smile on their mother's face amid her air of mock reproach. He's a hero, strong and bold enough to overcome any danger, invented animals and fantastic monsters included. He is not scared of anything. He has broad shoulders behind which we can hide or onto which we can climb to view the world from above. His is the surly frown in the face of small adolescent lies, which once discovered, require only a mother's intervention to bring forgiveness, with a stroke of the head and one last piece of advice, because you never know. He knows that *kids always have a rebellious desire to be disappointed by what has fascinated their fathers*, as Aldous Huxley put it. But then you grow up and you realize that your dad is dad, the one that we will all recognize in these telling illustrations and the words that accompany them, because at any time, he is there, the best dad ever!

"Fathers must always be giving if they would be happy themselves; always giving – they would not be fathers else."

– Honoré de Balzac

"A father has heart and arms so big
to bear the pain with a smile."

– Stephen Littleword

"Daddy, where does the sky end?
Why does the moon follow me home?
Where does the hour go in Daylight Savings?
Daddy, do I look more like you or Mommy?"

- Jessie Nelson, Kristine Johnson (I am Sam)

"When I grow up I want to be a little boy."

\- Joseph Heller

"I have a Father's Day every day."

– Dennis Banks

"A child on his father's shoulders:
no ancient pyramid or column is higher."

– Fabrizio Caramagna

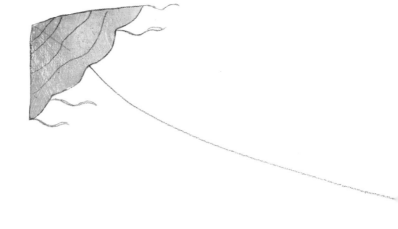

"I think the father-son love story
is a universal one which transcends color."

– Lee Daniels

"My father gave me the greatest gift anyone could give another person, he believed in me."

– Jim Valvano

"There comes a time when children detach their hands from yours, just as on a swing, when you push them for a while and then you let them go.
As they fly higher than you, the only thing you can do is wait, and hope that the ropes will hold."

– Paolo Giordano

"The truly rich man is the one whose children run into his arms even when his hands are empty."

- *Anonymous*

"It is easy to become a father,
but very difficult to be a father."

– Wilhelm Busch

"On the green they watched their sons

Playing till too dark to see,

As their fathers watched them once,

As my father once watched me."

– Edmund Blunden

"Be patient, answer every question that your child asks. That which today satisfies his curiosity will tomorrow contribute to a great treasure trove. The gems, coins and precious stones will be the knowledge acquired, and you, the parent, will have contributed to these riches. Start now!"

– Anton Vanligt

"It is a wise father that knows his own child."

– William Shakespeare

"One father is more than
a hundred schoolmasters."

- George Herbert

"Wise parents let their children make mistakes. It is good, once in a while, to burn your fingers."

- Mahatma Gandhi

"I am my father, second edition,
revised and expanded."

– Valeriu Butulescu

"There are only two lasting bequests
we can hope to give our children.
One of these is roots; the other, wings."

- Hodding Carter, Jr.

"It's a father's duty to give his sons a fine chance."

– George Eliot

"Being a father makes everything
in the world make sense."

– Cameron Mathison

"Being a great father is like shaving.
No matter how good you shaved today,
you have to do it again tomorrow."

- Reed Markham

"To hold a child in your arms
all you need is love, to raise him
you need much more, to be his father,
God needs to give you something."

– Elis Rapenau

"Every man can be a father.

It takes a special person to be a dad."

– Anonymous

"Being a father is a huge responsibility
but a satisfying one."

– Pierce Brosnan

"Dad is and always will be my living, breathing superhero."

– Bindi Irwin

"The prudence of a father is the most effective instruction for children."

– Democritus

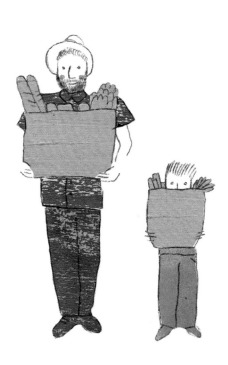

"It's just a wonderful feeling
to be a father and to have a kid."

- Richard Grieco

"The marvellous thing about being a father is to be able to look at your own child and realize that the universe is so much greater than you."

– Macklemore

"It's an ongoing joy being a dad."

— Liam Neeson

"Being a father fills me with wonder every day."

— Sean Pertwee

"I believe that we become what
our father taught us in the downtime,
when he wasn't concerned to educate us.
We are formed from scraps of wisdom."

– Umberto Eco

"A man's real riches
are his children."

- Francis Ford Coppola

"It is not flesh and blood, but heart
which makes us fathers and sons."

– Friedrich Schiller

"My father often took me to the cinema.
He told me about the first film he ever saw.
He entered a dark room and on a white screen
he saw a rocket fly into the eye of the Man
in the Moon. And there it got stuck.
He said that it was like seeing your dreams
in broad daylight."

– John Logan (Hugo Cabret)

"Father, even if you weren't my father,
even if you were an utter stranger,
I love you for yourself."

– Camillo Sbarbaro

"A father is always making his baby into a little woman. And when she is a woman he turns her back again."

– Enid Bagnold

"This is what it means to be good parents:
to show your child the ways of the world."

– Sophie Kinsella

"The heart of a father is the masterpiece of nature."

- Abbé Prévost

"Becoming a dad means you have
to be a role model for your son
and be someone he can look up to."

- Wayne Rooney

"He who begets a child is not yet a father,
a father is he who begets a child
and makes him worthy."

- Fyodor Dostoyevsky

"I cannot think of any need in childhood as strong as the need for a father's protection."

- Sigmund Freud

"I cannot think of any need in childhood as strong as the need for a father's protection."

– Sigmund Freud

"It doesn't matter who my father was;
it matters who I remember he was."

– Anne Sexton

"I have learned that when a newborn child squeezes his fathers finger for the first time with his tiny fist, he has him trapped forever."

- Gabriel García Márquez

"The relationship between father and son is more solid than with any team-mate. You can be frank with one another."

– Mario Andretti

"In that severity, and in the absence of doubt,
there was what his father had taught him
to father children, to be able to walk,
without looking back."

– Alessandro Baricco

"For a child, the father is a giant
from whose shoulders we can get
a glimpse of the infinite."

- Perry Garfinkel

ILLUSTRATIONS
Alain Cancilleri (Contextus, Pavia)

INTRODUCTION
Emma Altomare (Contextus, Pavia)

WHITE STAR PUBLISHERS

WS White Star Publishers® is a registered trademark
property of White Star s.r.l.

© 2017 White Star s.r.l.
Piazzale Luigi Cadorna, 6
20123 Milan, Italy
www.whitestar.it

Translation and editing: Contextus Srl, Pavia, Italy (translator: Louise Bostock)

ISBN 978-88-544-1124-1
1 2 3 4 5 6   21 20 19 18 17

Printed in China